I0617584

DARK

CLOVERS

By

Diana Dark

Copyright © 2021 Dove Bennett

All rights reserved. No part of this book may be reproduced or transmitted in any form or by any means, electronic or mechanical, including photocopying, recording, or any information storage and retrieval system without written permission of the publisher, except for the inclusion of brief quotations in a review.

Dove Publications, A Subsidiary of Dove Enterprise
www.dovebennett.com

Printed in the United States of America

This is a work of fiction. Unless otherwise indicated, all the names, characters, businesses, places, events, and incidents in this book are either the product of the author's imagination or used in a fictitious manner. Any resemblance to actual persons, living or dead, or actual events is purely coincidental.

ISBN: 978-1-7349956-6-4
Imprint / Publisher: Dove Enterprise

Cover Designed By Dove Bennett
Format and Layout By Dove Bennett
Interior Edited By Jessie Raymond

Table of Contents

* Part 2 of Aether Academy can be found in the sequel to Dark Clovers

Diana Dark

Aether Academy
The Start Of A New Story

Dark Clovers

PART 1

Deon started his day with extra excitement, brushing his large teeth until they were white as snow; they practically shone by the light of the San Francisco sun. He combed his soft, wild, black hair and put it up in a nice bun like he always did. Turning on the faucet water, Deon washed his face and cleaned around his ashy nose, clearing up his once tired-looking skin, revealing the smooth brown beauty beneath. He put on his new school's favorite polo shirt with the "A.A." logo written across it and tucked it into his nicely ironed black pants.

"Come now, Deon, your breakfast is ready. I don't want your food to get cold!" His mom shouted to him from the kitchen as she placed his food on the table.

"All right, I'm on my way," Deon responded as he quickly looked at himself in the mirror and headed downstairs. As he approached the kitchen, he could smell the wonderful aroma of the food.

"Excited about today, Deon?" his mother asked as she sat next to him and started eating. "Of course, it's not every day you get to go to an Academy on the moon. Especially one as prestigious as Aether Academy."

Dark Clovers

Deon smiled as he ate his meal in haste, eager to get to the space station.

"Slow down, it took me a while to cook this breakfast, and I want you to enjoy it." His mom said a bit sternly while still keeping a kind tone.

"Yes, ma'am," Deon replied.

He slowed down for the remainder of his meal, placed his dishes in the sink, and headed out the door.

"Wait! If you think you're leaving without giving me some sugar, you are mistaken."

His mom walked to the door where he was and kissed him on the cheek, hugging him tightly.

"I love you, my son. Make me proud."

"I will, mom. No worries, I got this."

Deon returned her hug and exited the house.

Taking the train to the space station was unusually comfortable on this day; it was usually overcrowded and consumed with a foul odor. It was a nice day. As he got closer to the station, he was in awe at the magnificence. He exited the train and proceeded through security. As he entered the spaceship, a kind stewardess provided him with a blanket and a pillow and got him to a seat. As friendly as the stewardesses were, they scared him a little because they were robotic with human faces. You could see the machine-like attributes because of the lines across their face. Also, the uniform they wore closely resembled a doll's attire.

Once he arrived at the Academy, he entered the grand hall where he saw hundreds of students gathering and conversing with one another, wearing the school's merchandise, smiling, laughing, and beaming with excitement. The doors to the grand auditorium soon opened, and they began to flood the room, taking their seats by each other, either by new friends or, like Deon, by strangers. The room was dark, except for the stage, where there was a spotlight centered on the podium.

A tall woman with pinned-up dark brown hair walked into the room. With the way she walked, it was easy to know that she had zero tolerance for nonsense while on the clock, but could kill at a karaoke bar after work. She took her place at the podium and spoke to them with a welcoming authoritarian tone.

The lady began with the words, "Welcome to Aether Academy."

Dark Clovers

The kids began to clap and shout as her words poured out, but she kept a stern look of silence, calming their rambunctious praise.

"Welcome, new students to Aether Academy. This school was founded in 1867 by Marcus A. Gray, a renowned educator and former philosopher. Gray was born in Greece and raised in Germany, where he mastered all seven factions of magical and supernatural powers, giving him the grand idea to spread such knowledge and skills across the world. In return, the world agreed to such teachings, and new scholars and philosophers were born from it. Gray was a very kind man with a great bristled beard and tall gray wild hair. He was said to resemble the American president Lincoln who, he admits, "flattered him a bit". As she stated the last few words, she slowed her speech down in a tone that expressed amusement towards him.

Then she continued, "But I digress... The school was an idea in the making for over 100 years. The advancement of knowledge and technological innovations made it possible for us to be here today. Now, in an orderly fashion, please exit the auditorium and head to the Gray Common Room where the organizers will hand you your supplies."

The doors opened, and students began to exit the auditorium to head towards the Gray Common Room, filled with sofas and tables. Standing on a small open

Dark Clovers

stage were two of the Head Organizers. They looked pretty odd to Deon, but that was probably because they were much older than he had imagined. The male organizer was a very stout man who wore glasses that made him look biggish, and he had a mustache that curled upwards at the ends. The woman working with him was a bit taller, and she had a beak-like nose with a skinny neck, but when you heard her voice, it was so sweet, almost as though she was singing to you. She wore conservative clothing, which complemented her nicely.

"Attention all first-year students! Please line up by the Golden rope where you will be assigned everything that you need for classes, including your schedules," the woman commanded.

"Names standing from A through H, please stand by the front, names that start with I through Q are in the middle, and then starting with R through Z is at the end," she continued as the students scrambled to get in their proper places. As it became closer to Deon's turn to get his schedule, his attention immediately turned to a beautiful student who was enchanting to him for reasons that he couldn't explain.

"Sir, please come up," the woman instructed as she held a list of names in front of her.

Dark Clovers

"Oh, sorry," Deon said as he realized she was speaking to him. He quickly approached her.

"No problem, name please?" she responded.

"Deon Mowoti," he replied with a smile on his face.

"Well, hello Deon, it seems as though I am your counselor. My name is Miss Temper," she calmly said while smiling back at him. She had dark black hair and snow fair skin; her eyes were hazel green, and she seemed like she had an hourglass figure. However, it was hard to tell since she was sitting down. She handed Deon his room key and schedule, as well as a bookbag of all the supplies he would need for his classes.

Deon headed to the group of elevators across the hall when he accidentally bumped into another student.

"Oh, sorry," Deon apologized as he helped pick up the boy's papers. When he looked up and saw him, Deon blushed a little.

"No problem, my name is Miles, by the way," his mate responded.

Miles was tall and had a spike of dark brown hair, and even though he had braces on his teeth, it only added to his handsomeness. His skin was light brown and clear. In addition to his appearance, he had a kind demeanor.

Dark Clovers

"My name is Deon", Deon introduced himself, smiling mildly to hide his nervousness. He looked at his new friend's key as he handed it to him and realized that they were roommates.

"Well, Deon, see you around, I guess."

Miles smiled at Deon, blushing as he got into the elevator with a group of students.

"What floor?" one of the girls asked.

"The 13th floor", Deon replied.

"Ha, that's funny. We are also going to the 13th floor. My name is Yasmina, and this is my roommate Katie."

Yasmina was tall and muscular with a more tom-boyish look than her roommate. Her hair was braided down to her shoulders and decorated with small golden rings. Katie was quite the opposite. She was of average height, cutely plump with rosy cheeks, and possessed long red hair tied back into a ponytail.

"Hi, I'm Deon. So, this is pretty exciting, isn't it?"

"Yeah, I'm so excited, but I can't wait to eat and scoop out some of the other fine selections that this Academy has to offer," Yasmina said as she looked at Deon with a flirtatious smile.

Once they reached the 13th floor, they headed to their respective rooms. It was at this point Deon learnt that the girls were his neighbors. He walked into the room, and found Miles changing.

"Want to grab some lunch with me?" Miles said with a friendly smile as he put on his shirt.

"Sure," Deon said before proceeding to change his shoes so he could head out the door.

"I'll be at the elevator."

"OK, be there in a sec," Deon said, trying to catch up with Miles.

Coincidentally, the girls came out and entered the elevator as well.

"Hey, Deon," Katie greeted, all smiles.

"Hey Katie, Yasmina, y'all going to lunch?" Deon asked as he stood comfortably between Miles and Yasmina.

"Yeah, you should sit with us," Yasmina proposed.

Dark Clovers

They all soon reached the cafeteria – the place was humongous. Different types of restaurants and bakeries occupied the room; it was also filled with tables and booths. Not to mention, the gaggle of students and staff whose voices filled the atmosphere.

"Where should we eat?" Miles asked, taken aback by the variety of foods available.

"A better question would be where should we sit?" Katie cut in.

Then from the corner of their eyes, approaching with a smile, was a waiter of some odd sort. It had blonde hair that banged to the side of its head, and its big anime-like eyes had a grayish-blue shine. The visible skin was a bit toned and smooth. It wore a waitress's uniform, but they weren't sure it was human.

"Hi, I am Clark. I will be assisting you today," it began. Almost immediately, it guided them to their seats and took their drink orders. Yasmina signaled Deon to sit next to her, and Katie sat next to Miles.

"We will have lemonade," Yasmina told Clark.

"I will have a sprite," Katie ordered.

"And I will have a coke," Miles added.

Dark Clovers

"Alright, I'll be back with your orders," Clark said as it turned around and headed out to get their drinks.

"How'd you know I'd want lemonade?" Deon asked with a smile.

"Lucky guess, I suppose," Yasmina smiled back at him.

Deon took out a book - more like a pamphlet of some sort - that gave him a brief description of magical and supernatural powers' seven factions.

Diana Dark

COLORS

OF THE

HEART

CHAPTER 1: THE LAST TO ARRIVE

At night, in a bedroom, where a boy was slumbering deeply, a chariot opened, and a tall, slender lady with black hair and pearl-like skin stepped out of a chariot and walked into the said boy's room. She silently glided over to the bed where the boy was quietly breathing and whispered something powerful in the boy's ear.

"It is time to go." She said softly.

The boy's eyes opened, and he saw the woman hovering over him as if she was waiting for him. He got out of his bed and took her hand. They both walked out of the dark bedroom into the chariot. With a wave of her hand, the chariot whisked them off to a secret place.

"Who are you, ma'am?" the boy asked respectfully.

"I am Lady Crescent, the torch of the moon. I am one of three. It has been my task to choose a child who has the potential to hold great power. Children like you, Corus," Crescent said as she looked at the boy's starry amber eyes.

After a moment or so, they arrived at the secret place, which appeared to be a mansion. The chariot door opened, and they walked out and saw the sparkle of a thousand lights decorated in a vast garden that surrounded them. Corus's eyes widened at the sight of it all, and as they continued their walk to the entrance, Corus saw other children walking with other adults to the entrance as well. Once inside the mansion, they were met by a host who looked a bit frightful to Corus. The man had black ram-like horns, and bovine legs and feet. He also wore a nice vest and dress shirt that was amber in color.

"Hello, and welcome to the Manor of Dreams. I am your host, Chester. Tonight, we will see if you have what it takes to become part of our family. The top three will be chosen based on who passes the three trials we will give you," Chester said as a door opened in front of them all.

"How will I know if I pass or not? What will happen to me after the test if I pass?" Corus said as he looked nervously at the door.

"Don't worry, Corus; I have faith that you will be exemplary," Crescent said as she put her arm around his back.

Corus walked through the door, as did the other children. They entered a room with a table in the middle of it. On top of the table, a note sat nicely. One of the kids picked it up and read it aloud: "A room filled with a shadow of despair; conquer the nightmare to exit this lair."

Suddenly, a dark figure came out of a corner and began attacking the children mindlessly. Corus was in shock at the beast's sight as it seemed free to create chaos and threw some of the children like lifeless dolls. The beast then turned its sights toward Corus and slowly walked toward him. As the beast came closer, Corus backed into a corner. But in the spirit of survival, he attacked the creature.

He clawed and mauled the creature until he thought the beast was dead. He rose above the beast's body and saw an opened door; he walked through it and started his next challenge. As he entered the next room, he saw mist-covered grass beneath him, and the door behind him disappeared. He wandered as he soon found out he was in a maze.

He felt the grassy walls around him as he tried to find a way out. He soon approached a fountain with a gargoyle statue atop it. Corus looked in the fountain and saw his reflection clear as day in the water. He saw his dark golden brown skin, his wild black curly hair and deep amber eyes. It was like seeing another person, and the other person was looking at him as well through the water. He soon heard a voice above his head; it was the statue sitting at the top of the fountain.

"Who are you looking at?" the beastly-looking statue asked.

"I see me, I believe. Is there something I should see?" Corus asked curiously.

"Look again," the statue instructed.

With that command, Corus looked back down and saw two big glowing pale green eyes. Corus became stiff as a log, and he felt his skin chill and harden like he was in the process of being turned to stone. As he looked at the sight of it, he felt a presence behind him.

The presence moved closer to him, but he felt like he could not turn his eyes away from the image in the water. He felt trapped, but with strong determination,

Dark Clovers

he pulled himself away from the fountain. With that act, a door on his left opened, and he walked through it. He entered the last room and saw three doors that each had a sign on them.

The door on his left side held a sign that said: "In this room, you will find something cold, and something dry."

The door in the center of the room said: "In this door, you will find a lion that has not had his first bite." The last door on his right said: "In this door, you will find the broken heart of time."

"What do these mean?" Corus asked himself. Suddenly, an idea popped in his head; he would listen to the door to get an idea of what was behind it. He first went to his left and listened to the door; there, he heard a blowing sound as if it was a storm swirling in there. He went to the center one and listened closely, and heard nothing but a faint breath behind it. Lastly, he went and listened to the door on his right. He heard a soft tick and passed the echoes of voices beyond it.

He waited carefully and ultimately decided to go to the right door. As he entered the room, he saw a mound of old clocks sitting on the floor, and just beyond that, he saw another door. He walked past the clocks, opened the door, and came to the realization that he had arrived at the common room of the mansion. He saw Lady Crescent standing with a smile on her face as he walked toward her, glad to be safe.

"Good for you to be the first three to pass the trials successfully. Each of you has shown a unique characteristic that has allowed you to pass such trials,"

Dark Clovers

Chester said as he walked to all three children and shook their hands.

"You will all be shown to your rooms momentarily. In the meantime, you can say your goodbyes to your guardians," Chester added as he walked upstairs.

Corus looked at Crescent and was a bit worried about what could happen if she left.

"I can see the worry in your eyes, Corus. I understand how you feel. It will be alright; you are a bright candle in the night. I am proud of you and will check on you when I am able to," Crescent said as she hugged him.

"How will I be able to call you if I need you?" Corus asked.

"Light a torch in the garden, and you will be able to contact me. Don't worry, you will be great," Crescent said as she waved him goodbye and floated away.

CHAPTER 2: THIRST IS THE WORST

Corus and the other two kids that survived the tests were escorted to their rooms upstairs by Chester. They met a hallway at the top of the stairs and were assigned rooms chronologically - from the first child who passed the tests to the last.

There were three doors which led to three rooms built specifically for each person. The first room on the left was given to the first child who had won, and in the room, it was like a throne room where the child's bed faced the door; the room had a dresser and a wardrobe on one side, and a grand window on the other. The room was golden and white - truly magnificent.

The second room on the right was given to the second child and was right across from the bathroom. Inside the red and silver-painted room was a bed opposite the door. Facing the wall on both sides of the bed were windows, and on the right side of it was a grand mirror which stood calmly straight across from a wardrobe, crowned with a thicket of roses.

Corus received the last door, and in his room, his bed faced the door. He had a domed window above the bed which created a spotlight effect. Painted black and bronze, his room contained a wardrobe that stood next to the door. Across from that, a grandfather clock ticked steadily, making a faint rhythm fill the space.

Corus walked in and closed the door behind him. As he got in, he went to sit on his new bed in this strange new place. The following day, he woke from his sleep by the sun's light over his head but struggled to leave the comfort of the covers that wrapped around him. However, once he got up, he went to his wardrobe to look for something to wear. He found a nice dark green shirt and some dark blue jeans to wear.

He walked out of his room and headed to the bathroom to shower with his clothes in his hands. As he approached the door, he smelled the sizzling breakfast downstairs.

"Mm, I smell bacon," Corus said as he opened the bathroom door.

After taking his shower and getting dressed, he went downstairs and saw a table prepared for all three of them. Corus sat near the center of the table to have easy access to the food presented to them. He put some food

on his plate and poured some orange juice into his cup.
Soon, he heard one of the other children come down. It
was a girl; she had lovely light caramel skin and long
curly red hair that had a slight orange tint to it. Her eyes
were also a brilliant hazel green.

"Good morning, I am Eve. You must be the boy
who came out a little while after me," she said as she sat
next to Corus, smiling kindly.

"Good morning, I am Corus, and yes, I was,"
Corus replied as he spread butter on some toast.

"Well, do you have any idea what will happen
today?" Eve asked while pouring apple juice into her
cup.

"No, but I believe it will be a very peculiar day,"
Corus said as he ate the toast.

Dark Clovers

Soon, the last child walked down the stairs wearing a white robe. He sat on the opposite side of the table across from Eve and Corus.

"Good morning, I am Eve, and this is Corus. What's your name?" Eve asked kindly.

"My name is Charles, and yes, I was the first to finish the trials. You're welcome," Charles said boastfully.

"You're full of yourself, say what?" Corus quickly said.

"What did you say?" Charles asked confusedly.

Eve began to giggle a little. Charles sneered at them but soon, he was interrupted by Chester, who came out of nowhere and handed out a unique list to the kids.

"The list will set you on a path of discovery, and when all is complete, you will be ready for the future task I have for you," Chester said as he opened the door to the backyard.

Corus and Eve walked out and observed the list, which recorded all tasks required of them. Meanwhile, Charles went back upstairs to get dressed.

"What does the list say, Eve?" Corus asked as they walked around in the yard.

"It says that we must enter the forest and find the blood of a tree undisturbed, the well of angelic tears, and the bowl filled with the…piss of a deer," Eve said cautiously.

"What of a deer?" Corus asked as he cleaned his ears out.

Dark Clovers

"The piss of one," Eve replied as they headed into the forest.

Corus heaved a sigh of disgust as he heard the voice of Charles running towards them.

"Hey guys, wait up!" Charles said as he caught up to them.

"You're late, but I would expect no less from someone of your stature," Corus said as he looked at the list.

"Well, perfection does take time. You of all people should know that third place," Charles said as he walked ahead of them.

Corus gave Charles a quick death stare but then calmed down and continued walking. Soon, they saw a great tree, and beside it, they saw an empty bucket.

"This must be the tree the list says we need the blood from," Charles said as he walked toward it. "Hmm, it seems we need something to puncture the tree so that we can get the blood," Charles added as he walked up to the tree and began to analyze it.

Corus walked to a side of the tree and found a faucet. He turned the faucet on carefully and watched as the blood of the tree-filled the bucket.

"I have the blood. Let's move out," Corus said as he proceeded to walk in their previous direction.

Eve soon followed, and Charles quickly ran in front of Corus to be the line leader. After maybe an hour or two, they found the well of angelic tears, and next to well, a vial sat there. Underneath the well, it said: 'A tear for a tear.'

Dark Clovers

"I think it wants us to cry in exchange for the water in the well," Eve said as she looked down and saw a filled well.

Corus drew the bucket full of tears while Eve took the vial and dipped it in the bucket, filling it with tears. Eve looked down at the well and cried over it, giving it back some of her tears.

"Good work, people, now let us head onward to get some…piss? Are you joking right now? I'm not getting any piss on me from some woodland beast?" Charles said as he brushed himself.

"Well, you're going to have to because I already got the blood, and Eve already got the tears. All that is left is for you to get the piss," Corus said with a smile.

"I bet you would love to see me get pissed from a deer," Charles said as he sneered at Corus.

"Pause, did you just say you want me to watch you get piss from a deer? Highly suspicious," Corus said, looking concerned.

"I didn't mean that…you know what I meant, third place! Let's just go, it is dusk, and I do not want to be here at night," Charles responded as he walked forward on their previous route.

A few moments later, they saw a deer, and it stopped to take a... well, you know, use the bathroom.

"There you go, Charles. And you may have to use your hands because I see no gloves, nor do I see a bucket anywhere, so I guess it is all you, buddy," Eve said as she sat down on a fallen tree.

Dark Clovers

"If I have to, I will for the greater good," Charles said as he walked over to the deer and put his hands under the deer's body.

They all waited for the deer to do its business on Charles' poor hands. All of a sudden, Charles heard a rumble in the deer's belly. The deer slowly lifted its tail, and brown bullets began to fly, and as fate would have it, the deer began to piss as well. Charles was so shocked that he could not move. He stood up with the piss in his hands and began to walk back to the mansion, but as he headed back, he did, of course, step in deer poop. Life is funny like that.

When they got to the mansion, it was night, and one by one, they walked into the house. First Charles, second Eve, and thirdly Corus. Chester was in the room, and in front of him was a big pot.

"If you would, please bring the items on the list," Chester asked as he lit the fire underneath the pot. Corus gave the bucket of blood to Chester, and Chester poured it in carefully. Then Eve came and put the teardrops in the pot, which made a puff of smoke appear. Finally, Charles came around and dumped the piss in the pot, changing the color of the liquid from pink to yellow.

"Now that all the ingredients are in the pot, and the moon is angled perfectly above, I believe we can start. Eve would you please come forth?" Chester requested as he signaled her to come to him. Eve walked over to him and waited for further instruction.

Dark Clovers

"Eve, take this spoon filled with the concoction made and drink," Chester said as he gave her the spoon that held the liquid inside.

Eve drank the liquid in the spoon and, after she was done, she walked back to her original position. Charles and Corus went up next. They drank from the spoon and then returned to their initial positions.

"Done before the great moon and pale sun, I call you three to awaken," Chester said with his hands held high.

Soon, a gust of wind flooded the room and embraced the kids viciously. A moment later, they also began to feel something activate in their body, filling them and emanating from their bodies. Charles had a golden aura around him, Eve had a red aura around her,

and Corus had a black aura around him.

They all were amazed by this power, and Chester

too was surprised with the outcome of their auras.

Nevertheless, Chester released them to their rooms and

told them that their lessons would begin the next day.

CHAPTER 3: ARE YOU READY?

The following day, Corus woke up to the sight of a group of tigers in his room. His eyes widened in confusion, and he carefully walked out of his room, making sure he did not step on a tiger. When he was entirely out of his room, he saw Eve's door open and heard the cry of eagles.

"Eve, where are you?" Corus asked as he looked around her room.

"I'm over here," Eve stated as she opened the door to the bathroom.

Corus looked back and was shocked to see Eve covered in feathers and with hair that looked like a whirlwind had been through it.

"I guess we both got surprises this morning," Corus said as he looked at her with the kind of 'what happened to you' face.

Suddenly, they both heard a scream from Charles' room.

"Help, please, someone save me!" Charles yelled as he laid stiffly in bed.

Corus and Eve opened the door to his room and saw a horde of snakes slithering around the room. A snake slithered across Charles' body, and Charles looked as if he was about to die.

"Stop standing there and help me!" Charles commanded as the snake slowly moved across him.

"Did you just command me? I don't think I can help you unless you say please," Corus said with a smile.

Dark Clovers

"What? I'm not going to say please to you, just help me!" Charles commanded as the snake kept moving closer to him.

"Until I hear you say please, I will just let the snakes eat you. Come on, Eve, let's go have breakfast," Corus stated as he turned around and started to head downstairs.

"Wait! Please take the snake off," Charles pleaded. Then the snake stopped and looked at him.

"Alright, now was that so hard?" Corus said as he walked in the room, picked the snake up, and tossed it to the other side of the bed.

Charles jumped out of bed and ran out of the room to the breakfast table. Corus and Eve walked down the stairs and saw Chester waiting patiently for them as he drank some tea.

"Hello, how did you sleep?" Chester asked as he sipped some tea.

"I was sleeping fine until I woke up in a room filled with snakes! I could've died; I almost was eaten by those beasts," Charles said as he fanned himself and drank some water.

"Oh, so your animals came in. Wonderful, now we can proceed with your lessons," Chester said as he put his tea down and walked away from the table.

"What do you mean, our animals?" Corus asked as he ate some bacon.

"After the ceremony last night, the universe, aka Buzzfeed, sent your spirit animal. The snake in Charles' room is the animal that he is connected to spiritually," Chester explained as he walked outside.

Corus, Eve, and Charles all walked outside and saw a training course. At the center, were objects that resembled similar things you could find in a store.

"Come and choose your anchor," Chester said as he presented the items in front of them.

Charles went up first and saw a mirror, a ring, and a necklace. He chose the mirror and went back to the line. With the mirror in his hand, he began to admire himself and fix his hair. Eve went up and took the necklace, which had a fully bloomed rose on it. Soon after, Corus went up and grabbed the black ring, which he admired greatly.

"Great, now that you all have your anchors, I want all of you to hit the target to your left," Chester instructed as he pointed to the left side of the yard. They all turned left and studied in front of the target. Corus placed his ring on his finger as Eve put on her rose necklace. They all faced their targets and waited.

"Are you all going to start, or do I have to show you?" Chester inquired as he stood waiting.

When the trio nodded for him to show them, he continued, "So here is what you do, focus on your target and then fire," demonstrating it on a nearby tree.

They did as they were told and began to fire. Charles started to aim his mirror at his target, and golden energy fired out, blowing through the target. With a smirk, Charles blew away smoke coming from the mirror. Eve followed behind him and shot what looked like red fire, and burnt the target. Corus focused on his mark, and the shot looked like black lightning, which made the target explode.

"Wow, guys, two thumbs up to everybody," Chester hailed them as he put two thumbs up and smiled. They went back in the house and into the library filled with talking books, chattering across the room to each other, laughing, crying, yelling, and gossiping.

"In here, you will learn more about your supernatural qualities and what you can overall do daily, when you are in a fight, etc.," Chester said as he floated around looking for their book.

"Ah, here it is. OK, so here are each of your books based on the auras that you have shown. Red for Eve, gold for Charles, and black for Corus. I would suggest you read up on your abilities immediately, so that you are prepared," Chester added right before he left the library and closed the door, leaving them inside.

They all started reading from their books and were intrigued by what they read. Corus read his book and saw that black auras were known to manipulate the factors of night, to astral project, and change their form into a cloud of darkness. If they wanted to, they could hide behind someone's shadow. With their connection at night, they could see everything, even in the darkest places.

Eve read her book about red auras and found that people with this type of aura were passionate and fierce. It said that red auras could manipulate all facets of fire and project them, and then they could turn into fire. With this connection to the fire, they could also burn souls -

good or bad - when they would touch the person if they wanted to.

Charles read his book and seemed highly pleased with what he could do. The book highlighted that golden aura people are usually good-hearted, but some can have a Golden aura and be vain or conceited. Golden aura people are connected to the Earth, the birthplace of gold. They can shoot a blast of golden light and turn their enemy into the goal with a single touch; they can also reverse the effects by touching the person again. They can turn into gold if need be during specific situations.

"I can turn myself into gold! Oh my, it is like fate wants me to have this glorious gift," Charles boasted as he investigated his mirror.

Suddenly, they all heard yelling and banging coming from outside the library. Eve went to the door and pushed her ear near the entrance to listen to what was happening. Soon, she felt a rumble and moved away from the door. Then Chester flew through the door and landed with his face facing the floor.

"You should have given up when you had the chance, kids. You're coming with me," a strange man said as he entered the room right after Chester. The man was tall and seemed brutal, and to add to that effect, he wore a dark leather trench coat and had a beaten down cowboy hat on his head. His eyes mirrored those of wolves, and he looked hungry.

"How dare you try to command me, you ruffian? Go now, and I'll spare your life," Charles said as he held his mirror firmly.

Dark Clovers

"Oh, is that right? Well, go ahead, hit me," the man said with his arms open.

"OK, you asked for it," Charles said as he faced his mirror toward the man and shot a golden bolt. The bolt barely did anything to the man, and the man kept walking towards Charles.

"Is that all you got, boy?" the man asked. "I'll show you what for!" Charles answered as he shot a giant bolt at the man.

The man bounced back a little. "That's what I'm talking about. Hit me again. Come on. You know you want to," the man said as he stood still.

"No, Charles, you have done enough. Leave him to me," Chester said as he ran to the man headfirst, tackling him into the next room.

Charles, Corus, and Eve ran out of the room and headed to the forest for safety. They ran past places covered by dead branches and leaves. They heard the howling of wolves behind them, and so they continued to run deeper into the forest. Unfortunately, they ran into a dead end, and the wolves were closely behind them.

"What are we going to do? They're going to kill us; They're going to kill me!" Charles said as he began to panic.

"Please, shut up. We are going to fight them. Now, if you happen to get hurt, it is fate," Corus said as he looked at the wolves that were fast approaching them.

They all agreed they were ready to fight, and the fight did come, but not in the form of wolves. It came in the form of the man, who had a jagged scar on his face.

Dark Clovers

"Hello kids, come quietly, and we won't have to get violent," the man said as he motioned towards them.

Then he began to form as the moon rose right above them.

"Stay back, or else," Eve stated as a firebolt formed in her hand.

"You're a feisty one, aren't you? Don't worry. I'll make you calmer," the man said as he began to turn into a giant 7-foot-tall werewolf.

The werewolf started to come closer, and Corus could feel a familiar sense of survival, as he walked in front of them both. His eyes glowed of pale green, and his body morphed into a large 6-foot-tall Tiger. They both stared at each other as I slowly got closer. When the werewolf became restless, he attacked the tiger.

The tiger dodged the attack and smacked the werewolf with his paw, and his claws sharp and out, cutting across his side. The werewolf began to bleed, and he whimpered a bit. The tiger saw an opening. With his great jaws, the tiger dug his teeth into the side of the werewolf and tore him apart.

Eve was a bit shocked by this, and fear curled around her. However, Charles squirmed behind her in total fear. The tiger looked at them, and then suddenly, it reverted into Corus. He wiped his mouth clean of blood and saw the horror in their faces.

"I don't know how I did it, but we need to go back to the house and see if Chester is dead or not," Corus said as he walked back toward the house.

Dark Clovers

Eve followed behind, and Charles ran past them both to the house. When they all got there, they saw Chester lying on the floor, dead.

"What do we do now?" Eve asked as she closed the eyes at Chester.

"First, we give him a proper funeral, and then we pick up the pieces from there, agreed?" Corus said as he set our piece on the wall.

"Agreed," Charles and Eve complied, with all three looking at each other in agreement.

CHAPTER 4: CAN YOU FEEL IT?

A red owl flew into the house through a window.
It set itself on a pedestal next to a grand chair. Sitting in
the chair was a man in a black coat, wearing worn-out
black leather boots and gray pants. His hair was black
and short, and his eyes were pale white.

"So, that is what happened to my Hunter. I knew
the children were strong, but I did not anticipate a tiger.
Oh well, that is why we have plan B. Huntress, it is your
time to shine. Bring me the boy and his friends, and do
not fail me. I promise, your punishment will be less
merciful than the werebeasts," the man said as he waved
his hand, and he and the owl disappeared.

Dark Clovers

"I will not fail you, my Lord," the Huntress said as she allowed a wicked smirk to come across her face. Back at the mansion, the three had already fixed everything that was broken. The three went outside to say their last goodbyes to Chester before he was set on fire. Eve walked up to the funeral pyre and put a few flowers on each side of Chester.

"We mourn you, Chester, and hope your soul is in a better place. I speak for all 3 of us when I say you weren't half bad. You were a good satyr," Eve said as she lit the pyre. Corus stood beside her, looking at the corpse of the fallen teacher.

Eve shot the flame, and the fire began to engulf the pyre and Chester. It felt like the right thing to do, the best way to honor the fallen teacher.

They all stood for a moment, and one by one, they entered the mansion without knowing the next thing to expect.

"Well, we still have our books. But the real question is, who sent that man?" Eve wondered. She brought the books into the room and laid them down on the table.

Suddenly, they heard a knock on the door. Corus walked to the door, and behind him, Eve and Charles were ready to attack. He opened the door and then saw a woman in a royal green pantsuit, trimmed in black and decorated in gold buttons. She had a hat to match; she held a cane in one hand and a purse in the other.

"Hello, I am Ms. Umbrake. I will be your new Guardian and teacher for the duration of your training." Having said that, she smiled and walked into the mansion, looking around to observe the area. She had a welcoming smile, and her eyes were ruby red. It was obvious that she had a youthful likeness to her - an otherwise mature demeanor. Her hair was dark brown like old tree wood.

Five luggage bags that were previously floating around fell behind her.

"I'm sorry, who sent you?" Charles asked as he looked at her with suspicion.

"No need to be sorry, my dear. The council sent for your previous teacher, and I should have gotten a letter three days in advance. Where is Chester? Is he still here?" She asked as she walked towards the kitchen.

"Oh, he died yesterday protecting us from a werewolf," Eve said with her head slightly tilted down.

"Oh my! Well, that is strange. This is even more reason why we should finish your training," Ms. Umbrake replied. Immediately, she sent her bags to Chester's room with the snap of her fingers.

Corus heard a tapping at the door. He opened the door, and the Raven flew in and sat on the shoulder of Ms. Umbrake.

"Hello, clever bird. Well, kids, the sun is hiding behind the mountain, and you all must be hungry. Go freshen up, dinner should be ready when you come down," Ms. Umbrake said as she pushed them upstairs and headed back into the kitchen.

All three went into their rooms and waited as the elders instructed them. When the three were done, they went back downstairs and sat at the table, which looked quite small, as if it were meant for four people and not

Dark Clovers

10. They sat at the table; Corus was across from Charles, and Eve was across from Ms. Umbrake's chair.

Ms. Umbrake walked in and sat in her chair, and with a snap of her fingers, plates filled with food entered and floated over to each one of them. When the meals landed on the table, they began to eat.

"So, how is everyone?" Ms. Umbrake said as she cut her steak.

"Fine, how are you?" Eve responded as she too ate her coal salad.

"Great. I mean, besides the fact of what happened, I feel great," Ms. Umbrake said as she ate her bloody steak.

"If you don't mind me asking, what were you up to before this?" Corus asked as he cut up his fish.

"I don't mind at all, my dear. Before I was put here, I worked as chief officer of the comet force, a faction in the Esoteric government's law department. They help keep order in the worlds and realms across the Earth and beyond," Ms. Umbrake replied as she sipped some of her drink.

When everyone had finished with their meal, they all prepared to go to their rooms, and with the snap of her fingers, the plates floated back into the kitchen. Corus, Eve, and Charles went to their rooms and went to bed. Downstairs, Ms. Umbrake shut her door and sat in front of her mirror. She took her hat off, and her slick brown hair flew down to her back.

She wiped her face with a wet towel and took off her gloves as her black gloves were reeling her soft and smooth hands. Her nails were perfectly sharpened and painted black. Raven flew toward her and landed on top of the mirror.

"Ah yes, I believe we should call him," Ms. Umbrake said as she walked to the center of the room. She then poured salt down on the ground, and made a circle.

"Sumo atum corpse," she chanted, with her arms crossed in an X formation. Soon, a green light appeared, and then it took a form revealed to be Chester.

"Hello Chester, I heard you died. That must be hard for you. Anyway, I was hoping that you would have left me with something to help finish the kids' training," Ms. Umbrake said as she crossed her arms and looked at Chester.

"How did you get in this house? Where are the kids? What have you done?" Chester asked, frustrated.

"Is that the thanks I get for taking these kids under my benevolent wings? Just because I'm evil doesn't mean I'm without range. I've been a caring and loving guidance for these confused kids," she said with a humble expression masked upon her face.

"You will not turn those kids to the dark. Their hearts are pure. Neither you nor your filthy master can dissuade them from the righteous path," Chester vehemently stated.

"I am disappointed in you, Chester. You should know that I am more powerful than their hearts, and the Lord of Owls should be mentioned in a respectful tone, lest you wish to be mute for all eternity. Well, good talk,

Dark Clovers

call you later," she replied as she smiled and waved goodbye to Chester.

Chester's spirit went away, and Ms. Umbrake went to bed.

CHAPTER 5: TIME TO MAKE A CALL

At midnight, while everyone else in the house was sleeping soundly, Corus was searching the house for a torch in his dark cloud form. As he floated around the house in the dark, he stumbled on a wooden mace.

"This could be used as a torch," Corus thought aloud as he looked at the mace.

He turned back into his human form and grabbed the mace. Then he walked over to the door and used the shadow next to it to go outside without making any noise. Once he was out of the house, he walked through the garden and soon made it to an area in the garden center. With a wooden mace in one hand and a match in the other hand, he made a torch.

He lifted the torch in the air and presented it to the moon. A moment later, Lady Crescent arrived holding a Lantern in her hand, made of blue light.

"Hello Corus, it has been a while since we've talked. What has happened with you and the others?" Lady Crescent asked as she knelt to see him at eye level.

"Chester died, and we have a new teacher," Corus answered as he looked at her with concern.

"Oh my...What is the name of this teacher?" Lady Crescent asked superstitiously.

"Her name is Ms. Umbrake; she said that she worked for the comet force for the esoteric government. Does any of this make sense to you?" Corus asked.

"Yes, I do believe I've heard of Ms. Umbrake working for the government. How is that possible, though?" Lady Crescent said, confused.

"What do you mean?" Corus asked.

"She died in the War of the Day. Her daughter, however, had tried to follow in her mother's footsteps and became chief of the comet force, but was fired by the law council due to her being in cahoots with the Lord of Owls," Lady Crescent explained as she looked around them.

"Who is the Lord of Owls?" Corus asked curiously.

"The Lord of Owls is a being who is almost as old as me. Like me, he too is a patron of night and all that it holds. He, however, wants to use his power to become a god. See, what you must understand is that there are three gods; the God of Day, the God of Night, and the God of Twilight. These three gods have been the shapers of everything we know. The God of Day and the God of the night are two sides of the coin, making them equal in status. The God of Twilight is the one who flips the coin, keeping the balance of both in place. The Lord of Owls wants to make himself a god who would cause an imbalance for the scales," Lady Crescent explained while looking at Corus in his eyes.

"What should I do?" Corus asked with a worried look on his face.

"You need to be very wary of his woman. She could be dangerous and still could be working for the Lord of Owls. I must go for the night calls. Stay vigilant,

Corus," Lady Crescent said as she stood back up and floated away to the moon far above.

In the morning, Corus sat at the breakfast table and waited patiently for the others. He patted down his wild, grassy, black hair and wiped the crust from his eyes. Ms. Umbrake came into the room, and white black and green silk robe flowed down to her ankles. She gazed around the room and was shocked to see Corus up so early.

"Good morning Corus, I didn't expect you to be up so early. How did you sleep?" Ms. Umbrake asked as she sat down in her chair next to him.

"I slept fine, although it is quite difficult for me to sleep with my clock ticking in my room," Corus said as he sat back in his chair.

Dark Clovers

"You'll get used to it after a while. I remember one time when I was a kid. I could barely sleep in my room because the wolves kept howling at the moon. My mother told me that it is in their nature to howl at the moon. It is not for us to command their natural duty. So, if your clock ticks, it is only a natural duty for it to do so," Ms. Umbrake said with a smile. She got up from her chair, walked to the kitchen, and started to cook breakfast.

Eve came down in her red hair which was fluffy and wicked. She slumped her way down the steps and sat her seat at the table.

"Morning Eve, how did you sleep?" Corus asked as he fixed his position to look at her.

"I slept like a baby. I thought I heard someone talking last night, but then I realized the wind was just rustling outside my window, so I wasn't worried," Eva replied as she fixed her hair.

"Good morning Eve, how are you, my dear?" Ms. Umbrake sat in her chair as she re-entered the room.

"I'm good, Ms. Umbrake. How did you sleep last night?" Eve asked as she began to yawn a bit.

"Well, I slept pretty well last night, although the real question is, where is Charles?" Ms. Umbrake curiously asked as she looked at them both.

CHAPTER 6: HONEY IS SWEETER THAN GOLD

As they all sat at the table, they began to wonder where Charles could be. All 3 of them went upstairs quickly and knocked on his door.

"Hello, it is time for you to wake up, my dear. Breakfast is on the table," Ms. Umbrake said as she knocked on the door.

She knocked again and heard nothing. She opened the door and saw that he wasn't in his bed. All three of them walked in and searched the room. They even looked in his wardrobe but still didn't find him.

Ms. Umbrake looked around the bed, and Corus looked around everywhere else. They all found nothing except for some golden scratches around the window.

Ms. Umbrake looked around the window and took out a strange type of magnifying glass. It had a wooden handle and an oddly-shaped top made from a peculiar old metal. She saw through it and found the cause of the golden scratches.

"I see what has happened here. There was a struggle, and someone took him. By the golden marks, he must've turned himself into gold rather than shooting golden bolts. Someone stole Charles, and I think I know a way to bring him back, that is, if he is still alive. But don't worry, in his form, he's completely safe," Ms. Umbrake said with a smile as she walked out of the room.

Corus and Eve followed and walked downstairs with her.

Dark Clovers

"You two need to get dressed and meet me down here in exactly 3 minutes. Go off. Your time starts now," Ms. Umbrake said as she waved them off.

Corus and Eve quickly got dressed, walked downstairs, and stood there waiting for Ms. Umbrake in her pantsuit that had the prominent color of the green and black pattern. She held out a pocket watch and looked at it intently.

"We are ready to go," Eve stated as she presented herself in her lovely flowing ruby dress; wrapped around her waist was a silver bow with ruby heels to match.

"You are looking quite fetching, Miss Eve. And look at you, Mr. Corus, such a nice black vest with pants and shoes to match it, and what lovely royal blue dress shirt. My dears, I am impressed. Now let's go," Ms. Umbrake remarked as they walked outside to the porch. Ms. Umbrake took out a silver feather and formed a bubble around it.

"Here is a lesson for you, my dears, silver is the wife of gold, so the only way to find our golden pupil is from this feather made out of pure silver," Ms. Umbrake said as she wrapped a chain around the bubble and them.

Soon, they were wiped off in the direction of where Charles could be. Far off where the air was smooth like the river beneath it, a group of mountainous barbaric warriors headed toward a campsite where they held various treasures gathered from the worlds near and far.

Dark Clovers

"Hello, someone help me! These beasts are going to kill me! Help!" Charles yelled as he was carried in a box to the campsite.

"This statue speaks a lot. Korgo! Get some sweet cane so we can shut its trap," one soldier said as he set the box down.

Korgo came to wrap the sweet cane around Charles' mouth tight, causing him to mumble his words, and making him inaudible.

"That's better. Where did you even find that thing?" the leader asked as he started the fire.

"We found that on Earth. Yeesh, that place is crazy. It isn't like what it used to be. They are so strange. It feels like the humans have changed in some odd way," Korgo said as he sat around the started fire.

"Well, be glad we don't have to go back there again. After tonight, we won't have to go back there at all," the leader said as he laid back and closed his eyes.

The sun had dipped in the ocean, and the moon had come out of the mountain.

On Earth, Ms. Umbrake and the children had found a cave entrance beneath a great tree in Siberia. As they went into the cave, they found a great wooden door.

"Oh dear, well, if he is behind this door, then we have truly lost him," Ms. Umbrake said as she put her head down and shook it.

"Why, what's behind that door?" Eve asked curiously.

"Well, the door leads to a place where there are beings who don't take kindly to mortals, especially humans. Sadly, Charles is human, and he is gold. Both things can get you killed," Ms. Umbrake said as she analyzed the door.

"Well, can't we just sneak in the place and take him back? He is still needed, I guess. Or maybe we should just let him be," Corus said as he looked out of the cave.

"No, we can't. We have to go in there and save him," Eve stated with a serious tone.

"You know what, Eve, I think you're right; you and Corus go ahead first, and I'll follow behind," Ms. Umbrake said as she stepped away from the door.

"Alright, let's get this over with," Corus said as he went to the door and turned the knob.

He could feel so much power emanating from the door. When he opened it fully, he saw a whole new world rich with life and lit by moonlight. As agreed upon, he and Eve walked through the door, and Ms. Umbrake followed behind them, closing the door behind her. Then she wrapped a red bow around the knob.

They all began to walk into this new world, and as they continued, the world became a thick jungle in the night with only the silver feather guiding them. After a while, they found a campsite, and, in a cage, they saw Charles sleeping with something wrapped around his mouth.

"He seems so peaceful. Maybe we should just let him rest," Corus whispered as he looked around the campsite.

"Sadly, we can't but, we can free him before the captors wake up," Ms. Umbrake whispered as she messed with the lock. After a moment or so, the lock unhinged, and she could open the door to the cage.

She shook Charles awake, and because he was surprised to see them, he almost made a noise of excitement, but Eve signaled him not to make any noise. Once he was out of his chains and the sweet cane was taken off his mouth, they all started to go.

"Hey guys, I don't want to freak anyone out but, where are the captors?" Corus asked as he looked around the campsite.

Soon, they halted and looked around them, and, in the bushes, red eyes gleamed toward them, and they all moved back slowly. As they moved back, they bumped into something behind them. When they looked back, they saw a brutal man towering over them, holding a club in his hands.

"That's not good. Well, let's go before something worse happens," Ms. Umbrake said as she pulled the kids closer to her.

But as fate would have it, Charles shot a golden bolt, and it made the barbarian mad.

"Really? We're going to die. You've killed us. I hope you know that," Corus said as he shook his head. But then he remembered he had powers and created a shroud of darkness that blinded everyone.

"Everyone hold onto me," Corus said as he pulled them out and jumped in a shadow.

Soon, they all appeared at a temple not too far from the campsite and began to observe their surroundings.

Dark Clovers

"Where did you bring us? This place is so dusty and full of who knows what in here," Charles said as he brushed himself off.

"Well, suck it up. We are at least away from those people," Corus curtly replied as he looked around. "Well, look at that. We are in a temple," Ms. Umbrake clarified as she walked up to a statue.

"How do you know it is a temple?" Eve asked, walking up from behind her.

"I know because this statue is of a god of some sort," Ms. Umbrake said as she started putting her hands on the statue, observing it.

They walked through the halls of the temple and found no one. Then they found the courtyard where they saw a person cloaked, kneeling under the moonlight, praying.

"Hello, don't be afraid. We were wondering where we were and thought maybe you could assist us," Ms. Umbrake said as she stepped closer, but only a little.

"What do you seek?" the person asked.
"We seek a way out of this realm back to our own. Will you help us?" Ms. Umbrake replied, getting much closer to the person.

"How many are you that seek this?" the person asked.

"There are 4 of us," Ms. Umbrake replied as she called the kids to come.

"As expected, but sooner than I thought," the person said as she took off the cloak's hood, revealing a woman who had long flowing black hair, and skin, which shined like rich copper. Her eyes were like diamonds.

"Who are you?" Corus asked.

"I am Betronia, and I am the queen of the forest," she said as she stood tall and mighty, truly showing her statuesque body.

"Wow, you are tall," Corus said in awe.

"We have no time to waste, the barbarians are here," Betronia said as she heard the yells of the barbarians near them.

They all followed her and ran toward a door that appeared out of nowhere. It opened wide, and all of them got to a whole new realm. It was beautiful. As the sun creeped out of the sea, giving birth to dawn once more, the realm of the forest was basking in its light.

"This is my kingdom, Forestra, and you are welcome to all its beauty," she said as she presented her kingdom to them.

"That is fantastic, and I really am impressed by Your Majesty, but there is still the matter of your expectation of us. How did you know we would be there? Quite the coincidence, don't you think?" Ms. Umbrake stated suspiciously.

"The Oak mother foresaw that you would end up there, but I wasn't sure when. It's no mistake that destiny has brought you here," Betronia replied as she looked at Ms. Umbrake with understanding.

They walked off to the capital of the kingdom, and on their way there, they were met by royal guards - who were as tall as trees - that escorted them to the capital. As they reached the capital, they found a field of beehives that took the shape of church bells. Just beyond that, a river full of lily pads that sang soft songs flowed gently down the river. Once they crossed that, they finally reached the capital; there, everything was more prominent in person.

Corus, Eve and Charles were amazed by the cohabitation of both man and nature living in one harmonic kingdom. People were walking around, doing things common for them, like selling mushrooms big enough to wear, just like hats, or food that smelled sweeter than candy and tasted better than sugar. People rode on creatures covered in moss, and above flying in the air were birds of mammoth size.

They all walked through the doors of the castle, and in the very center was a stream that circled itself infinitely, never wavering and never drying. Beyond that was the throne where the queen took her seat.

"You three are important in ways you do not know, at least not yet," she said with certainty.

"My queen, she calls you and asks that you bring the children as well," a shaman said as he knelt before her.

"Alright, children, follow me. Madam, I will have to ask you to wait here," Betronia said as a door opened on her right side.

"OK, make sure they're back in one piece, my dear," Ms. Umbrake said as she encouraged them to go with the queen.

They all walked through the door, and it shut right behind them. When they were in the room, they saw a mighty tree decorated by light on its leaves. At the base of the tree, a woman sat calmly.

Dark Clovers

"Hello Oak mother, I have brought the children as foreseen," Betronia said as she knelt before her.

"I know this, my daughter. Good morning children, I have been waiting for you for a long time. I am the Oak mother. I was born with the gift of foresight, and my life and power have been tethered to this tree for centuries. You all are here because there is a man who seeks to use your power for his own. If this were to come to pass, the life of all realms would be threatened," she said as she looked at them with her glowing gray eyes.

"What are we to do, Oak mother? How can we stop this man from threatening us? Who is this man even?" Eve asked, obviously concerned.

"One of you knows who this man is. It is up to that person to share with others. As for the other question, you must go back to Earth to prepare for such a day. We cannot waste any more time, Betronia. Take all 4 of them to the door to Earth. Their journey has just begun," Oak mother said as the door behind them opened.

They walked to the door, and Ms. Umbrake turned to look at them.

"Are we ready?" Ms. Umbrake asked. As a response, the children shook their heads in agreement.

"Please stand back. I am about to open the door to your realm," Betronia said as she outlined the shape of the door.

Soon, it appeared and opened to the front yard of the mansion.

"Well, thank you for the hospitality, and I hope to see you again," Ms. Umbrake said as she walked through the door with Eve and Charles behind her. As Corus started to walk through the door, he was stopped by Betronia.

"Boy, listen well. I sense someone near you who may threaten your destiny. Be vigilant," Betronia warned, looking down at Corus.

"I will, thank you, and goodbye," Corus said as he turned away and walked through the door.

He was the last to walk through the door, and once he did, the door disappeared.

Diana Dark

THE FIRST *BLOOD* *QUEEN*

CHAPTER 1

In the country called Mediir, there was a young, kind princess whose name was Derna. However, by the eyes of the kingdom, her name was Your Highness, fourth in line to the throne of Fayne. She was a timid and quiet little girl who kept to herself most of the time, mostly avoiding her less than holy brothers. She had three brothers; the eldest was Prince Mord. He was, in fact, the greediest out of the three. He desired riches and didn't care about how he got them. He would stroll through the kingdom with a small group of soldiers and bully people around for whatever coin they had, and as a small trophy of his "success", he melted the gold pieces down and plated them on his teeth.

The second eldest brother was Prince Vino. He was disgustingly lustful. He would throw private parties with people masquerading in masks, performing shameful lust-filled acts under the guise of the night. He lusted for anyone and everyone he could get his soft and mischievous hands on except for his own family, of course. Well, at least his immediate ones, as his cousins took a deep shine to him whenever they would visit. People just seemed to be powerless against his charm, especially when it came to his alluring scarlet eyes.

The last brother was Prince Bartel. He was undoubtedly the vainest out of all of them. He had mirrors decorated across his room so he could see his face at all times. He was practically in love with himself. The one thing he prized most of all was his long golden flowing hair. People in the kingdom were not only jealous of his beauty, but were also enchanted by it.

These three princes were prepared to be king and were willing to kill each other for it. But, that all changed when the youngest of the royals arrived abruptly on a cool summer night. Princess Derna was a joy to have in the kingdom. She had long curly black hair, deep green emerald eyes, and her skin was a nice brown color, like the dark amber that shined in the earth. She was quite the spectacle. As she grew up, she admired her mother, Queen Fayne, and the power she wielded. Her mother, in return, took great favor in her, seeing as she was the only daughter she had.

One day, Derna was walking through the halls of the red marbled castle, taking the usual route near the gardens. She heard light chattering behind a group of large hedge walls, so she decided to see who it was and went into the hedged field. What was waiting for her was pretty disturbing. It was all three of her brothers seemingly taking advantage of a servant girl.

When Derna saw this, she was shocked by such a heinous act. She watched this and stepped back, accidentally crushing a twig. Though the sound was heard by many, only one brother saw where the sound came from and whom. Prince Bartel saw Derna run off back into the castle.

No doubt, a scheme fell upon his mind about how to handle the little interloper. So in the evening, he summoned Derna to his room for a small discussion. Derna entered his room and was a bit worried about why he had called her there.

Dark Clovers

"You called for me, brother?" Derna asked.

"Yes, I did. Tell me, sister, what did you see in the garden today?" Bartel asked as he combed his hair in the mirror.

"What do you think I saw, brother?" Derna replied, moving further into the room.

"Well, whatever you thought you saw, or have seen, forget it. Trust me, sister, it is best for you to be able to forget things like that if you wish to live here, or at all. You may leave now," Bartel said as he looked at Derna with a smirk.

Derna left the room, and something tickled her spirit. After hearing her brother threaten her, she felt angry and frustrated. She had never felt such feelings before and didn't know how to handle them, so she planned a "gift" for her brother. At dinner, when all of the family sat around the table, she felt it was time to spring the trap. Therefore, she reached under her seat and pulled from it a pie. She casually walked over to her brother and, with great delight, slammed the pie into his face.

She had a great laugh out of it. Vino and Mord certainly snickered about it as well. However, Bartel was outraged.

"You impudent little brat!" Bartel said as he was about to slap her.

"Enough! Derna, go to your room now, and don't come out until I give my express order," the queen said as she looked at them both in disappointment.

Derna ran to her room and slammed her door shut. She jumped into her bed and screamed in her pillow. Moments later, she slowly sat upright in her bed and calmed herself down.

"All in a day's work," She smiled.

The following day, she got dressed in a lovely blue skirt as usual. When she opened the door, a bucket of pig's blood fell all over her. She was speechless, and when she looked back upwards, she saw all three of her brothers standing there, smiling and laughing. In Mord's hand, there was an empty sack. Bartel and Vino grabbed Derna and dragged her into the sack.

"Let me go, you heathens!" Derna said as she kicked and screamed.

"This is a lesson I'm certain you won't forget," Bartel said as he and his brothers rode their horses into the woods nearby.

When they reached a dark part of the woods, Mord threw the sack on the ground. Derna crawled out, still covered in pig's blood.

"Have fun playing with the wolves sister," Bartel said as he rode off.

"Yes, have fun," Vino echoed as he too, rode off.

All three of them had left her at the mercy of the wolves in the woods. As suspected, a pack of wolves had already smelled the blood. They now looked to devour whatever was the source of the blood. Derna started to try to find her way back but was lost. However, the wolves laid close in the shadows. One wolf walked out in front of her and began to growl at her.

Derna slowly stepped away from the wolf until another came up from behind and growled at her as well. Before she even realized what was happening, Derna was surrounded by the wolf pack. She was indeed at their mercy. She picked up a large branch and held it like a spear. She swung frantically, making sure they kept their distance from her. Then with a swift leap, a wolf attacked her. Falling back, Derna impaled the wolf by accident.

Derna was at first horrified, but then she became excited. She kicked the wolf off the stick and looked at the other wolves, with her eyes looking hungrily at the rest of the pack. The wolves began to attack, and one by one, she killed them with a wicked grin. Drenched in the blood of the pack, she took the wolves' bodies and drove them into each other on the branch like meat on a pike.

She finally returned to the castle. On getting to the dining hall, she threw the unit of wolves on the table where everyone was sitting.

"Thank you for the lesson, brothers. I think I finally have the message you wanted to convey," Derna said as she walked off to her room.

Dawn came early the following morning, and screams could be heard from Bartel's room. The guards quickly arrived to check the source. They opened the door only to find Bartel completely hairless. He had become bald, and his face was naked, for not only did his hair from his head disappear, but his eyebrows as well.

Bartel became wildly distraught and, in his great depression, killed himself with a piece of a broken mirror in his room. The funeral was quick and grim, and looking down at him from above his grave was Derna, coldly staring at his empty husk.

"One down, two left to go," Derna said as she smirked at her brother's grave.

A few weeks later, the castle began operating like it used to, and this particular night of all nights was no exception to Prince Vino. He had one of his annual parties prepared, and it went according to his shameless plan. People became drunk and erotic, becoming free-flowing to sways of desire and lust. When the party ended, and everyone was asleep, Derna walked in, disguising herself with a beautiful mask made of amber.

She snuck into the bed of her brother, and with a sharp, clean knife in her hand, she cut off his primary accessory, which so happened to be in between his legs.

He was highly intoxicated and couldn't feel a thing.

Derna left, and when the morning came, the people on the bed with him woke up to a dead body. News of this spread, and another funeral needed to take place the following day. This time, when Derna attended the funeral, she was a bit preoccupied, thinking of what she could do to her eldest brother. Across the graveyard, a boy captured her eye. He was quite handsome for a peasant, and she was coming into her beauty gracefully. So for a short time, she was distracted from her goals, and it was lovely. They decided that instead of coming up with a plan by herself, they would plan her last brother's death together. She was very much in love with the boy after that, but wasn't sure if he loved her back, so she decided to ask him one night while they were in her chambers.

Dark Clovers

"Tell me, Bartemus, do you love me truly?" Derna asked as she looked at him curiously.

"Forever, you are my heart's one true desire Derna," Bartemus replied, kissing her on her forehead.

"The trap is ready, my love. All I need you to do is deliver this message to Prince Mord. Do you think you can handle that?" Derna inquired, smiling at him.

"Of course. No job is too hard."

Immediately, he took the letter and went to find the prince. When he saw the prince, he gave him the letter as instructed.

Mord looked at the letter with pleasure and headed out to the woods as the letter instructed.

"The treasure should be around here somewhere," he said as he scrambled to find it. When he saw the treasure box described in the letter he opened, poisonous snakes jumped out and struck him when he looked into the box. He died lying in the forest with venom choking his body and no one around to hear.

Days went by, and long after, a hunter found Mord's body lying in the dirt. The hunter went back to the castle and told them what he saw in the forest. Just like that, all three brothers had died in less than a month. Now the only one left in the castle was Derna and the Queen.

Derna was pleased by this new arrangement of mother and daughter; this was a new beginning. Days became weeks, and weeks became years. Soon, Derna was finally reaching her full physical maturity. She grew taller and became more defined in many areas, like her voice. For example, it wasn't as soft as it used to be, but it indeed became more commanding and quite seductive.

The vital thing to remember is that she was still in love

with Bartemus, who by "miraculous" means became

captain of the royal guard. Their affair was a secret for a

while, until the Queen began to suspect Derna. Derna did

not like this new watchful eye and conspired to make a

coup against her mother.

By the time the last bell rang the next day, the

Queen had fallen. Waves of sadness spread across the

kingdom, including in Derna's heart. But it had to be

done. The Queen would never allow a non-royal to court

with a royal, especially an heir.

Regardless of this, she still dealt with something

quite dangerous that had been brewing for a long time.

She had begun to manifest powers of a particularly

destructive and perhaps corruptive nature. These powers she had came from some dark place deep within her and festered uncontrollably and unknowingly.

The day following her mother's death was the day of her coronation to become Queen of Mediir. Draped in gold, sapphire, and rubies, Derna ascended to the throne and made it possible for her and Bartemus to marry one another.

CHAPTER 2

Being Queen was a bit rocky at first, but she handled the pressure with Bartemus by her side. Bartemus would be able to do a lot more if he was king, but since he was not born of royal blood, Bartemus could only be the prince. He was a contemptuous and caring man to his wife and his people, and though he was born a peasant, he still had the heart of a leader.

Humble yet strong, Baremus portrayed kingly traits, which allowed him favor amongst the nobles and other royalty that would visit from time to time.

Bartemus truly and wholeheartedly loved Derna. She was his angel, his muse. Nothing could come close to her, not even the gods that gave him breath.

She was his everything until the rumor of her power spread to his ears. They claimed that she was not mortal but instead, a monster. He had to test the truth of these rumors to understand better what she could be, so in the night, while the Queen slumbered, he cut a piece of her hair and traveled in the cover of darkness to the tower of the court wizards. There, he ordered them to make proof of whether or not these rumors were true.

"I am to know whether I married a demoness or I have married an angel," Bartemus spoke with worry heavy on his breath.

The wizards tested and revealed to him the truth about the Queen. "Her Majesty is divine in blood as you know all royals are. However, it is tainted by darker powers boiling and bubbling up in her, spreading

Dark Clovers

outwardly. If she has not shown any abilities by now, they will erupt soon," the wizards warned Bartemus. The next day tested everyone when a criminal came into the court, and the Queen herself was the judge.

"Are these accusations true?" Derna asked, rolling her eyes in disgust.

"No, Your Majesty, I would never do such a thing," the criminal replied, bowing his head in respect. "You're lying! You did kill them. You're a monster," Derna said, looking at the man, aware he was lying. "I'm not, I swear," the criminal cried as he looked up at Derna.

"You dare look at me. You seem to have forgotten whose presence you are in. You have forgotten your place!" Derna fumed as she squeezed her hand into a fist and her emerald eyes began to glow.

Springing from the man's chest were black roots that spread quickly all over him, and his body began to wither like he had all the life sucked out of him until he was an empty husk of skin and bone.

"Clean this up," Derna ordered as she left her throne room and headed toward the gardens.

Derna strolled around the grand garden and ran her fingers lightly over the flowers. She began to think about how things used to be when it was just her and her mother before her powers sprung. After she had killed her idiot brothers, it was like a golden age of life. She missed her mother and it was sad that she had to kill her.

Dark Clovers

"If only she didn't question me. Well, we can't all be as respectful of privacy as others," she thought as she picked up a thorned rose.

"Your Majesty, I have troubling news," her handmaid who interrupted her soliloquy said, bowing to Derna.

"Well, out with it. What is this news?" Derna asked while admiring a flower.

"There are four armies at our borders and four princes in your throne room who wish to speak with you," the maid said as her voice trembled a little. Derna immediately walked back toward the throne room, where four princes stood lined up in front of the throne.

"I apologize I kept you waiting. I had no idea that you were coming," Derna said as she curtseyed in respect.

"We have arrived to discuss the fact that you have no allies and the fact you are without an heir. We are here to rectify that problem," one of the princes explained.

"Well, I am sorry to disappoint, but I am in no rush to bear a child. As for allies, my kingdom is rich in both resources and wealth. Also, we have a pretty good army and prefer to stay neutral. As you can see, for those reasons, none of you are needed," Derna said as she sat on her throne.

"We can see, but war comes to all as it has come to us. You are the barrier between our kingdoms, and whoever has your kingdom as an ally will be sure to win," another prince replied.

"What, pray do tell, would happen if I were to refuse all of you?" Derna asked.

"We would take the kingdom by force and divide it evenly among us," the last prince said as he slightly unsheathed his sword.

"I see. Sadly you leave me with no choice but to execute you," Derna said she gestured to the guards to shut and lock all the doors in the throne room.

The princes looked confused and unsheathed their swords. Derna aimed at the princes with her hands outstretched toward them, and bolts of dark energy shot out, killing the princes where they stood, leaving only ashes.

"Now, to handle the armies," she said to herself, satisfied with what she had done.

Derna headed toward a tower, and when she reached the top, she grabbed a telescope and looked through it to see where the armies were.

"There you are," Derna said as she put down the telescope. "They will learn that the Queen of Mediir is no one to be trifled with."

Afterwards, she lifted her hands to the sky, and her emerald eyes glowed brightly. From above, storm clouds formed above her. Waving her hands, the dark clouds circled the borders of the kingdom, and then as the winds came in, the storm clouds took the shape of wolves that came down on the armies and tore them to pieces.

Dark Clovers

She stopped the attack and sent in small squads to kill the rest of them, except for one person from each kingdom. She told each of the survivors from the kingdoms to return to their kingdom to inform their rulers that their princes were dead, and if they attempted to attack her again, they would surely perish.

The survivors obeyed their orders, and days later, four messenger birds came to the castle with a message of peace. Sadly, due to these events, the people of Mediir, whom she loved, feared her terribly. Some even desired to rebel against her. When she heard this, she was heartbroken. Soon enough, thoughts of rebellion became words and rallies, and then it became an army.

"They wish to rebel against me. To take what is not theirs. Then they also must wish to die. It is time to let the beast free," Derna stated as she gave the signal to her guardsmen. "Where is Bartemus? You'll soon see."

Deep in the rebel's camp, a group of royal guards arrived and with them was a cage covered in curtains. The leader of the rebels stepped forth with his sword at the ready.

"What is this? What has the witch queen brought?" the leader asked.

"This is a gift from Her Majesty. Enjoy," the royal guards said as they left the cage and went back to the castle.

The leader of the rebels went to the cage and pulled down the curtain. When he did that, he also opened the cage. In it was Bartemus. He had become a great tall man with a scar on his right eye, holding an ax. The man swung his ax and killed the leader and went through the camp, killing anyone he saw. Like a wild beast, he tore through the people, blood flooded the ground, and screams echoed out to the sky; the rebel forces were crushed.

Derna received news of the camp's destruction and was pleased. She decided to retire in her room and rest for the night. She changed her clothes and opened her window to let the light of the moon shine in her room. She went to bed and shut her eyes, clearing her mind of all the events of the past few weeks. Climbing in from the window, a rebel from the camp that had escaped the others' fate drew his bow and aimed a black iron arrow, and then shot it into her heart.

She woke up instantly and killed the archer with a blast of dark energy. She died right after she killed him.

She laid on the bed lifeless, and her blood sneaked out

from her chest where the black arrow was.

CHAPTER 3

As a funeral took place for Derna in the land of the living, her soul slowly fell into the pits of hell.

"Deep down, I always knew I'd end up here. I just didn't think it would happen so soon," she thought as she arrived closer to the brimstone gates. When she landed, she began to observe the area around her, and there was hardly anything but fire and chaos.

Derna arrived at the wide gates of hell and walked through them. Waiting on the other side of the gate was a demon disguised as a butler.

"Who might you be?" Derna asked as she walked toward him.

"I am here to lead you to your torment," the demon replied.

"I would prefer to meet the ruler of this realm," Derna said as she observed the geography around her.

"As you wish," the demon replied as he rang a bell. Once he rang the bell, a ship came through a portal of fire, decorated with bones and blood. Derna got on the boat and, with the demon's guidance, traveled to the castle of chaos: the house of the King of Hell.

Once they made it to the wide doors, Derna came off the ship and knocked twice on the door. The knocks echoed heavily, and on the other side of the door, a massive creature came galloping toward the door, shaking the ground beneath. Then from behind the beast, a voice called out, making the creature retreat to wherever it was before. The doors opened, and Derna

Dark Clovers

entered the castle's grand hall and headed straight down the hallway. Sitting casually on his throne, the King of Hell observed Derna as she came closer to him.

"So what does a sweet creature like you want from me?" the King of Hell asked, intrigued by Derna.

"A sweet talker, how nice. I am not here for pleasantries; I want to leave this place immediately. You're going to allow me to leave or face the consequences," Derna dared as she looked at the walls decorated by beautifully horrific portraits of both man and monster.

"Who do you think you are? A god? I'll let you leave my castle in peace, but recognize that I am in charge here. Leave my presence mortal."

"Alright, if you won't let me leave willingly, I'll just leave by force. See you soon," Derna said as she left the castle and began her conquest.

She became a wild creature, like a great wolf devouring souls for power. She wreaked havoc and hysteria throughout the realm. Then it finally came for the time for her second meeting with the King of Hell.

"So you have finally come back to try to leave?" the king asked as he stood up from his throne.

"I have," Derna replied as she looked at him and her emerald eyes glowed.

They both shot beams of energy, and the collision of power shook the castle.

"Enough of this. You will die," the king warned as he transformed into a dragon.

Dark Clovers

Derna grew angry, and with her wicked powers, she transformed into a great wolf. The king blew hellfire at her with great ferocity. But that meant nothing. She focused her energy into a howl unlike no other. The roar blasted right through the king, and he turned to ash from the inside out, becoming dust in her wind.

With the king defeated, she became Queen of hell, and with the mantle of power, she resurrected herself back to the land of the living. She clawed out of her grave and breathed in the open air of the earth.

"I am back. After all this wretched time, I am back," she said as she looked out into the world she had left behind.

Diana Dark

THE SLICING

Dark Clovers

'Outstretched our hands. Down then, we pray. Eyes closed shut, hearts open, no need delay.'

In the orphanage chapel, the children prayed, as the head nun, Mother Margaret, watched them with a keen eye and calmly paced with her black cane aiding her walk.

"Time to start our activities children, rise from your pose and proceed outside," Mother Margaret said as she guided them to the open door.

During this time, the kids played outside on the swings, in the grass, but one particular little girl relaxed in the shade of an old twisted tree. Her name was Anaid. Her eyes were a sweet brown, and her skin, a rich dark amber color. Her hair was curly and thick, and black as night to add to her shine. She spoke with a sweet, kind voice to the tree, and if you watched her, you would think the tree spoke back due to her mannerisms. However, just across the field was her brother Brailen who mirrored his sister, but instead, had hair that was a bit more wool-like. His eyes had a beautiful shade of silver. Unlike his sister, he preferred to be barefoot, feeling the earth between his toes as he played in the mud.

Night soon came, and after the children had their supper, they retired into their rooms. Like many nights that had come before, a dark spirit came to haunt them all. Some kids even screamed on occasion. However, when the spirit came to Anaid's room, it would converse with her until the light of dawn would come, after which it would disappear from the room. Some nuns who

Dark Clovers

walked past her room on some nights could hear the creature talk to her and reported this to Mother Margaret.

One morning, Mother Margaret pulled Anaid to her office. She protested to Anaid that conversing with dark spirits was devilish and must never happen again. She told her that she needed to pray twice as hard every day. Well, one thing led to another, and Anaid walked out of the office with bloodstains on her shirt. Mother Margaret was surprisingly dead; she laid out on her desk, unrecognizably so.

Other nuns that worked there buried Mother Margaret and started to advertise for free adoptions as much as possible. As luck would have it, a very wealthy couple had come and adopted Anaid, as they saw how pure and ultimately adorable she was. Her brother

Brailen was adopted by a fine British couple and taken back to England. There, he lived with them in the British countryside.

Anaid lived happily with her adoptive parents. She was taught by the best tutors around, and as the months went by, she became quite knowledgeable for such a young girl. She spent some of her time with her parents. Other times, she went into the grand garden they had. At the center of it was an old twisted tree like the one at the orphanage. She was overjoyed to see it, and just as she did at the orphanage, she spoke to the tree extensively.

Soon, winter had come, and it was Anaid's first Christmas with her new family. Luckily for her, she also experienced her first party since her parents had an annual party on Dec. 27th. It was nice to meet her parents' friends, and the party theme was "Masquerade", so everyone had masks on. It was a sight to behold.

Tapping his glass lightly, her father summoned everyone's attention and stood confidently at the top of the stairs. "Welcome, and thank you for coming. Now that the side festivities are concluded, it is time for the main event, the thing we have all been waiting for - the ritual of the lamb. We have eagerly waited for a prime dish to be served for a new grasp of longevity, and here she finally is."

The crowd turned their sights to Anaid as she smiled, waiting to see what was going on. Needless to say that she soon found out that she would be the sacrifice. They brought her to an altar set neatly under the twisted tree at the center of the grand garden.

Standing above her, with her eyes that seemed to be

calm, were her adoptive parents, and in her mother's

hand was the ritual knife. With a swift strike, she killed

poor Anaid.

Her soul was wrongfully condemned to a realm

of great dark power. Still, on her arrival there, she had

aged to her prime, and also, unknown to those who

sacrificed her, they had unlocked a force unlike any

other. With that said, she clawed her way back to her

body, and then she arrived back in her body, a fully

grown woman.

Anaid stood at the table, and everyone was

amazed. She snatched the knife from her chest, which

healed instantaneously. Then like a preying wolf

amongst sheep, she began to slaughter those that

Dark Clovers

attended the ritual ruthlessly. After she did, the snow that

covered the garden was colored by the party guests'

blood. She watched her adoptive parents look upon her

with horror running across their face. She walked to face

them and, with her bloody hands, reached into their chest

and pulled out their hearts. Holding their hearts in her

hand, she smiled wickedly and proceeded to eat them.

She proceeded to eat like Halloween candy, as though it

was her reward.

As if naturally acquired, a beautiful black dress

that was long and misty appeared on her body. Her hair

was flared up like black fire, and her eyes were still

sweetly brown but added to this, was a richly hungry and

intense look which her eyes gave like a lion on the hunt.

Her body was full and statuesque. Her nails on her hands

and feet were at a medium length, drenched in a black gloss and were as sharp as daggers. Her feet, once covered in blood and snow was now dressed in pointed black heeled shoes.

As she surveyed the grounds, a barely living party guest squirmed around.

"Oh, look what we have here, a wayward soul scrambling frantically for life? I can save you, but in this exchange, I want you to do something for me." The person shook their head in agreement, and Anaid healed them, but when she did, she whispered something in their ear that made them run as fast as they could away from her. By the time the police showed up, it had already been too late. Anaid had left mysteriously, leaving the party's bodies laid out neatly in the snow spelling her name.

Dark Clovers

Word of such a killing began to spread around.
Soon, more and more reports of horrific killings and a
mysterious woman behind them began to pop up. This
created many stories and names for Anaid, like the wolf
witch, the demon in the dark, etc. Like many stories that
faded into legends and myths, Anaid's didn't.

A year had passed, and a new couple entered the
house. By this time, the house itself looked abandoned
and withered down. It was understood that the couple
were renovators and were going to stay in the home
temporarily for about six months. As fate claimed them,
they had a child, and their stay in the house was pushed
to about a year and six months. Contracts were signed,
and assurances were made to keep the family in place for
the 18 months promised to them. The family made the

home their own while still keeping in the idea of its
modelization and innovation.

"Good morning dear, ooh, the house smells good.
Whatcha cooking?" Henry said as he placed his head on
his girl's shoulder.

"Breakfast, I know how you get when you don't
have any, and I'm not in the mood for it, troublemaker,"
Gladys smiled as she kissed his cheek.

"Well, call me down when you are ready. I'll go
check on the baby," Henry kissed her on the head and
went upstairs, and headed toward the baby's room.
As he walked towards the room door, the door creaked
open before his hand touched it, signaling to him that it
was already opened. He walked into the room, and
looked around to see if anything was amiss. When he
found nothing, he proceeded to walk to the baby, still

Dark Clovers

asleep and gently kissed its forehead. As he left the room, he felt the soft breeze across his neck as if someone was breathing behind him. He quickly turned around and saw no one there.

Henry walked back downstairs, and his wife called him to the kitchen to eat. They sat down next to each other, smiled and talked for a while. Shortly after, they heard the baby cry.

"You go ahead eat. I'll check on the baby," Gladys said as she walked away from the table and headed upstairs toward the baby's room.

As she approached the baby's room, she heard the sound of another voice singing to the baby, calming it down.

"Outstretched our hands, down then we pray,

eyes closed shut, no need to delay."

Gladys breathed heavily on the door, and the air from it made it creek just a little. When she looked into the baby's room, she found no one but the baby standing in its crib with a smile. She walked through the door, headed toward the baby, and held it up.

"Who were you talking to?" Gladys said as she held up the baby. Blind to her sight, Anaid stood right behind her and breathed calmly on her neck. When Gladys turned around, Anaid vanished instantly. Gladys went back downstairs and finished her breakfast, and soon got to work on the house. Days had passed, and like a thief in the night, Anaid always spoke to the baby. Her voice could be picked up on the baby monitor.

Dark Clovers

Gladys would listen and sometimes walk over to the room where her baby was and tried to catch the voice but would fail. However, one night, Gladys thought herself to be clever and set a trap for the voice. Anaid came as she always did at precisely 12:12. Gladys was hidden under a cradle, quite uncomfortable at first, but adjusted the longer she was there. Anaid began to speak but then stopped as she heard someone else's heartbeat in the room.

"It seems we have a visitor," Anaid said. Then she bent down to look under the bed and found Gladys sweating profusely as she looked at her. Their eyes met, and it chilled Gladys to the bone.

"Well, what a nice surprise, Gladys, is it?" she jested. Anaid took a step back and took the baby in her arms, and then cradled the child gently.

"I have a wonderful Idea. Let's play a game, shall we? It's called how much pain can a baby take without waking up."

Gladys scrambled to get out from under the cradle. While she struggled to do that, she looked at Anaid in anger.

"Let go of my child," Gladys spoke sternly.

"Shhh, you don't want to wake the baby," Anaid creepily smiled at Gladys while rocking the baby.

"Let's start. I can take its nose," Anaid said as she plucked the baby's nose clean off without the baby even wincing.

"I can take its ears," she continued.

Dark Clovers

Anaid plucked its ears, and little by little, each part she plucked clean off disappeared somewhere around the house.

"Now, it's your turn to play. Find the baby's parts, and put it back together. You better hurry, time is ticking. You have till dawn to make it whole, or else it'll be my baby."

Anaid left, but before she did, she gave Gladys the naked, faceless head of the baby. It was still warm because the child was still alive somehow. Gladys and Henry frantically searched around the grand house and thankfully found all parts of the baby before dawn's light. But this was an experience they never wanted again. So, they left the house that very same day.

Diana Dark

DR. MORTON

Dark Clovers

PART 1

Hello mortals, and welcome to my glorious story. I am

Eresabith Morton, but most people call me Doctor. I was

born in a small town in Scotland called Breighlan. The

date of that glorious day was 1705, March 3. The sky

was ripe in a storm, and I slept quietly in my mother's

bosom.

However, more people were in that room other than my

mother, but she couldn't see them. One of the other

people there was my godmother, Frelon. She was and

still is quite mysterious. She appears very selectively,

and when she does appear, she always keeps to herself.

Regardless, this is about me. My childhood was

beautiful, I was always running wild around the woods

near my house and feeling as though I was nature, and

nature was me. That all changed when my father came

back from his long trip from some awful and dank place.

He often spent most of his time at the pub with his

charming "friends".

After he came back into my life, things went in a

direction in which I was not quite prepared for. I did all

my usual activities, like walking through our little

garden and picking the flowers to make small crowns,

getting water from the well down the dirt road, and

walking through the woods. One day, I must've come

into the house at the wrong time because he scolded me

for tattering up my dress, which I had made clear to him

was for my outdoor activities.

"Look at your dress. You muddied it up. You think we

can afford for you to always get dresses every day," he

Dark Clovers

scolded with a heavy scent of mead fleeing from his
mouth.

I looked at him confused as to why any father would
scold their daughter about something so trivial.

"Father, I know we don't have a lot of money, but mother
said it was alright to play in this dress," I replied, ever so
sweetly.

"Well, my word goes above your mother's, and what I
say goes, and I say that you best not play out there in the
woods again with any of your dresses," my father stated
sternly.

I left and went into my room, and shed a few lost tears,
then calmed down. From that day on, I chose to stay
inside to wear my dresses freely, without anyone
stopping me. As I got older, I became more solemn due

to the changes I was going through; my hair grew longer and turned a dark blood red color. My skin became toned and fair, freckles decorated my face and developed quite excessively.

My beauty was almost at peak bloom. Sadly, I was not the only one who saw this. My father, with all his brilliant ideas, thought it was best for me to meet his "friends". So when I was 16 on the dot, he took me to meet his friends. It was utterly predictable.

He thought it would be nice for me to entertain his friends for profit, but I, of course, knew that this was never going to happen. So, when I was toying with them and laughed at their drunk jokes, I found it quite convenient that not only was there a sword, but also a gun sitting comfortably by my side.

Dark Clovers

I, at that moment, did what any rational person would do; I fired the gun at the man in front of me, slit the throat of the man behind me, and then proceeded to stab my father multiple times in the chest. All the other men around me stood back, but one, who did not quite get the message, tried to attack me, so I stabbed him in some exciting areas.

My lovely amber eyes shined in bloodthirst, but were soon quelled at a moment's notice. The other men I did not kill didn't stay to ask me questions; best if they didn't, I really wasn't in the mood. I walked outside and took a fine black stallion - one of the dead men rode in with my rightful prize.

I burned the bodies of the deadmen with the help of a convenient torch lying around, in respect, of course, for the surrounding animals. I didn't want them to get sick off the mead rotten bodies. That's just the kind of caring person I am. Anyway, I rode back home to my mother and told her of the terrible news, in spurts of course, so that she wouldn't think her daughter was some crazed murderer.

The poor lass was taken for a minute, but in all actuality, she was grateful to finally get rid of that oh-so-great man. Time progressed, and I grew into the great vessel I am and always will be today and forever. Although, when my mother died, it did take quite a hold on me for a good while, I've stayed faithful to her wonderfully loving example, that no matter what happens, I can and will persevere.

In 1727, I got a job as a nurse and spent most of my time around my godmother, Frelon. I rarely speak about her

Dark Clovers

because she is overly mysterious and secretive. She lived in a small cottage deep in the wilderness, where there was no one to keep her company except for me, when I visited her and the creatures around her.

When I had come to live with her for a few months, it was like living in a lucid and abstract dream. She did strange and unusual things but what was more shocking was the revelation she bestowed on me, one bright, calm day. Frelon and I walked down a woodland path that soon became dark as we entered deeper into the aching, haunted woods.

I was very uneasy in that wild place. I could feel the air lay heavily on me, making my chest feel as though there were stones on top of it. I started to faint, and then I did.

When I woke up, I found myself lying on a great stone and wooden table. There were four other people around me, standing stiffly next to my godmother, who stood proudly in the center of them all. They all dressed in white, which was very cult-like.

"What is happening?" I asked exhaustively.

"We are here to awaken your spirit, my dear," Frelon said as she appeared to hold in her hand a silver and emerald dagger.

"Are you mad, because you seem to have lost your mind?" I replied as I looked around the area.

"No, my dear, just stay still. It'll be over real quick," Frelon said as she raised the dagger above my heart.

At that moment, I knew this crazy cow was trying to kill me. They held me down, and in the blink of an eye, my godmother struck me in the heart and released this

155

ridiculous power within me. After seeing that nothing terrible happened to me, I made the sensible decision to kill her and everyone else because, *you just don't do things like that with your godchildren.*

I leaped up from the table and proceeded to break the neck of one; then I took the dagger from my godmother and killed the rest of them, but when I was about to go to kill her, she had vanished. I kept the sword and walked back to the cottage to see if I would find her there, but my search was in vain. She had completely and utterly disappeared.

One funny thing that happened that day was that I was mugged by some d-rate thugs, who then stabbed me multiple times. I thought I had died, but it turned out I was immortal, or perhaps that I had become immortal

due to my godmother.

In 1785, I moved to England. I lived there for quite a

while, and obtained high prestige in my own right;

through medicinal and archaeological practices. In these

studies, I made many cures for illnesses such as

smallpox and the flu. My loyal assistant Percilla worked

with me on many of these discoveries. Still, she did the

occasional housekeeping for me as payment for living

with me.

On a Sunday in November of that year, I was invited to

the queen's ball, and going with me was, of course, my

servant/ right hand, my darling Percilla. Now, you should

know that Percilla was a short girl, well, at least, to me if

we're comparing my 6 feet to her essential 5'5 height;

she had blond hair, blue eyes, and pale white skin. You

Dark Clovers

can imagine the struggle to find something that one

could do that could make that poor girl.

Nevertheless, her value to me was very apparent at that

time. When it was time to go, I told her not to embarrass

me in front of the queen's court. As I walked in, I graced

everyone with my presence in my emerald and black

dress with a black veil covering my face. I remember

when she told me she understood not to embarrass me,

and I believed her until she screamed "bloody murderer"

at the queen's ball and had to be carried out by the court

guards.

Sadly, I had to do what any good and caring person

would do in that situation and disown her as fast and as

calmly as possible.

"Goodness gracious, what a hysterical display. I would hate to be associated with someone of such dramatic and uncivil antics," I said with the utmost care for her.

"Quite indeed, glad that such rabble is weeded out," one of those pompous inbreds stated.

After the ball was over, I walked outside to find my Percilla standing quietly and in deep thought.

"Do you feel better?" I asked her.

"I do, my lady," she replied.

"This will never happen again, correct?" I asked.

"Yes, my lady," she said as she curtseyed humbly.

"Good, let's go home," I said so simply and walked into the carriage that had arrived for us.

We went back home, forgot all about the matter, and continued with our standard medicinal practices. After some months, I had a chance to go on an expeditionary

Dark Clovers

adventure with a few other fellow researchers I had

contact with over my long life span. Our discovery laid

in Siberia's dark land woods, where a rare item had been

said to have laid there.

This discovery would have indeed brought my status up

significantly, giving me the title of the greatest woman of

archaeological studies in the world. How so, you may

have asked. Simply because this item was no ordinary

trinket of a dead king or lost world? No, it was much

more than that. In fact, It was a godly weapon of legend.

It was said to give anyone worthy enough the dominion

over death itself.

When my team and I went to Siberia to find this

legendary weapon, we encountered several challenges.

We came closer to obtaining it. The first and least

shocking of these challenges were animals, of course,

bears especially, since they were highly territorial. Due

to this factor, one of us ended up being killed by one.

So now, a party of five became a party of four. We

progressed, and the challenges became increasingly

complex and continued to come as we came closer to our

discovery. When we were nearly there, our discovery

team went down to two people; me and my closest

colleague, Dr. Froe Winston.

He was very handsome and tall but a bit submissive. I do

dislike weakness, but it was a bit cute on him. However,

when it came down to both of us, he did show growth in

character. He became more protective of me.

Nonetheless, we reached the weapon, which was

surrounded by statues of solid warriors. I walked toward

the gun and found it quite unique. It was a tremendous

Dark Clovers

one-sided ax with multiple carvings decorating it and strange words scribed on its hilt.

"Wait! You don't know what will happen if you touch it," Froe said with a worried voice.

"You're right. You should do it, just in case something happens. You wouldn't want anything to happen to me, would you?" I asked, making my eyes starry.

"Of course not. I'll do it," Froe said as he attempted to lift the ax.

Sadly, due to his unworthiness, he was killed by one of the statues. I, however, lifted it and was not harmed at all. In fact, I merged with it, and ever since that day, I've been feeling exceedingly better than most people.

Well, that is how I, Eresabith Morton, claimed the title: "Goddess of Death." Don't worry your little heads, I am just here to take some of your cares away. Stay ready, my

dears, for part 2 of this lovely and glorious story all

about me.

PART 2

Hello mortals, and welcome to PART 2 of my glorious story, I have had some complaints, but as a whole, I've been a benevolent saint to those poor unfortunate mortals.

Let's start in the year 1813 - America has been official for a moment, but I know I am not the only one who feels like they shouldn't have won. Regardless, I took a ship there and was impressed by this New World. Percilla, my fateful pup, did as dogs did and whined the whole way through. She was so grateful that I loved her because she would have ended up in the ocean, dining with the fishes, if I didn't.

When we arrived at the Boston port, I met this very

handsome boatman named Seamse Frutnin. He helped

Percilla and I with our luggage. He was rugged and

robust, and his smile was almost as perfect as mine. The

only thing I didn't like about him was his fish smell.

Although this may have been an obstacle, I preferred to

quickly deal with it, so I could proceed with getting to

know him better.

For the next few weeks, I spent time together with him,

and I even had time to feed Percilla once in a while.

Well, I'm joking. She always knew when dinner time

was. But I digress. My time with Seamse was terrific.

Each night's overflow of passion gave us an avenue of

love explored in each intimate, but ever so calm, meeting

between us.

Dark Clovers

These feelings, I couldn't explain. They fell from the heavens like rain. Joy and warmth captured me so, and in his golden eyes, a warming glow. I was so happy and felt what seemed like joy, and then it happened. He asked me to marry him, and I, without a second thought, said yes, and was eager for the wedding day to come.

It was chaos planning it, and it didn't help when people couldn't follow simple orders. But, like all things, they were quickly disposed of like dolls who had outlived their worth. The day came, and my heart raced as I walked down the aisle and stood face to face with my true love.

"I promise to cherish you, in all your wonder, my love. Through wind and storm, always," Seamse said as he looked profoundly and kindly into my eyes.

"I promise to love you until the end of time when all the world seems dark. I will be there for you," I said as I looked at him through my white veil.

"You may now kiss the bride," the priest stated.

He lifted my starry white veil, and we embraced each other in a fiery kiss. It was so strong, it warmed my perfect heart. At that moment, everything was perfect.

The years after that were wonderful. We had two children, one boy named Brailen and one girl named Galitan. Percilla was the nanny; she was thrilled to help raise the little ones. I guess she knew that if she outlived her usefulness, I would have to "let her go" - gently, of course. That way, she could go knowing that she had fulfilled her purpose. But that didn't need to happen, so everything was good.

Dark Clovers

As my children grew older, they showed significant developments of supernatural gifts passed down from me. Brailen had excellent navigational skills, and Galitan excelled at botany. This also meant that they were immortal too, but their father, however, was not. He grew older as we were young and beautiful forever. Every day, it became harder to see the man I once loved grow old and brittle. The day finally came, and he died at the calm age of 85. That is the one thing that I cannot stand. To see someone suffer. At least he died calmly and not in pain. I still sometimes think about how he used to tell me how he wanted to follow the sun into the ocean. So, as his final wish, his funeral was on a boat that sailed into the sunset: nothing but the best for my dear.

I struggled to handle the grief, and my children were also utterly devastated. Shattered in mind, my son joined a gang of pirates. He had seen them arrive at the Boston port and asked to take part in their barbaric adventures. I forbade him to do it, but he snuck out anyways and later ended up being killed by a sea witch.

My daughter hid herself away somewhere, never to be heard from again. She, on occasion, would send me letters but would never tell me where she was or who she was with. Those events told me two things: my children are not as immortal as me because I cannot die whatsoever. Two, Percilla is a faithful woman because she was there for me when they left.

I believe I have started to tear up. I am afraid we must cut this story short, my dears. But do stay tuned for part 3 of my glorious story.

Dark Clovers

PART 3

Welcome back, my dears, to Part 3 of my beautiful story.

We come to 1910, and sadly, at this time, my most loyal

servant Percilla has died. I prepared a funeral for, and

only I attended, for I knew not of her family. To be

honest, she barely spoke about her personal life. So I set

out to find her family, and dead end after dead end, her

family was nowhere to be found.

Work around my house was more than usual. Percilla

kept everything running like a clock, and knowing how I

am, I didn't really feel like doing work beneath me. She

cooked for me, cleaned the house, organized my

documents, etc. She was utterly irreplaceable, but you

know I have always found a way to replace even the most important people in my life.

I went, however, in a state of mourning. I became an aggressive alcoholic and slept in my now hollow and desolate home exceedingly too much; however, in the second year of mourning. I received an invitation to a small get-together. Highly idiotic, but it was something to do.

So I got dressed in one of my dresses that had a checkerboard pattern and was colored black and red. I put on my black veil and headed out to the party. When I arrived at the house, I was met by a burly man. He had a jagged scar placed on his right eye. Quite alarming, but it was far better than seeing a dead body.

"Dr. Morton, so glad you could make it," the host said with a smile.

Dark Clovers

His name was Barrell. He was a very round man, and his name must have been a deliberate choice by his parents. He was pretty wealthy as well as very joyous. There were others there, and of course, I felt so awkward. It had been a while since I had left the house, so being around people was strange for a minute. "I welcome you all to this little get-together. As is tradition, I will recite a poem from my collection," Barrell said as he took off a book from his bookshelf. I really didn't want to hear his voice, all I wanted was the wine, so while everyone was entranced by his words, I snuck into the kitchen to find some wine but instead found my new servant.

She was an African girl with exceptional arbor brown eyes. Her hair went down to her shoulder, and her clothes were quite tattered.

"Girl, what is your name?" I asked as I moved closer to analyze her.

"My name is Aliah," she responded.

"So you can speak English. Well, do you like working here?"

"No, ma'am," Aliah replied.

"Good, neither do I. Grab a bottle of wine and walk with me out," I said as I got a bottle for myself.

Aliah did as she was told and came with me with her bottle in hand. She seemed a bit nervous, but I really didn't know why. Then again, she didn't know who I was really. We quietly walked outside through the backdoor and hopped in my carriage.

Dark Clovers

"Things are going to change for you, and to start, we need to get you better clothes. You look so horrid in that thing you're wearing."

Aliah looked confused at first, but after our talk in the carriage, she got the memo, I think. The very next day, I took her to get tailored for her dress sizes. Surprisingly, she was only a few sizes bigger than Percilla.

I just had all Percilla's clothes stretched out to fit Aliah. From there, I personally taught her all she needed to know about how to not screw up my stuff. She learned exceedingly fast and did all her chores with outstanding merit. She did so well I thought it would be nice to take her out on a trip to New York City.

I was amazed at her facial expressions at all the sights she saw, and when we went to the theatre, she loved it so much. I felt proud of this. We stayed at a hotel for our

nights there. It was called the Corazon Cup. Very classy

and neat. The staff was terrific, even if they were

vampires.

Most people would look at this as a problem, but I was

widely known in the vampire community as the Goddess

of Death. She, however, was not accustomed to them.

One night, I was in bed reading, and I had noticed that it

had become late, and Aliah had not returned.

I got worried, and before I could get dressed to go out,

there was a knock on the door.

"Who is it?" I asked suspiciously.

"It's Aliah."

I opened the door and found her covered in blood.

"I'm sorry, I didn't mean to do it," Aliah said as she ran

to me and hugged me.

Dark Clovers

I embraced her and calmly asked, "Where is the body?"

"I don't know, I blacked out for a while, and then I woke up on the side of the building," Aliah said with a shaking voice.

She had been turned, but not by a bite; she had been manipulated into drinking the blood of a head vampire, for only the blood of the head vampire could turn someone by making them drink their blood.

I was furious with the situation, but not with her. So, we stayed an extra night. I had time to find the head vampire and was about to kill him.

"Any last words, beast."

"Wait, don't do this, can't we come to an arrangement?" The head vampire pleaded as he quivered with fear.

"I think you lost all chances to talk to me when you turned my assistant into a child of the night." I stood above him with my ax in hand, but before I could let the ax fall on him, Aliah killed him.

I was surprised, but you can only mess with someone so much until they snap. When she killed the head vampire, she had actually gained all of his power, and that was a lot. Given the fact that there are four vampire lords or head vampires, she had killed one and accidentally became one in the process.

Aliah and I had to leave that night, and so we did. We made it to Boston in record time. When we made it to the house, I had a talk with her.

"Aliah, now that you're the queen of vampires, you have more responsibilities now, and you will have people that will look up to you."

Dark Clovers

"I never asked for this. How am I supposed to live if I can only go out at night?" Aliah said with a sad voice.

"I am always a step ahead of you, my dear. Here, drink this," I gave her a potion I had concocted in my younger years for if something like this happened to me.

She drank the potion, and to her, it seemed as though nothing happened to her.

"What was that supposed to do? I don't feel anything," Aliah said, confused.

"That's good. That means it works," I looked at the window, and it was dawn.

Aliah looked at the sun and saw that she wasn't burning up and was excited.

"Thank you, Madam Morton. You are truly amazing," Aliah said with a smile.

"I know," I patted her head and headed upstairs.

"Bring my stuff up to my room when you have finished enjoying the light."

"Aren't I royalty? I don't have to get your stuff anymore," Aliah thought.

"I can still kill you."

"Good point, I'll be right up, Madam," Aliah replied as she got the luggage and brought them upstairs.

Well, that is the end of Part 3. There is always more to come. Yours truly, Dr. Morton.

Dark Clovers

PART 4

Hello my dears, welcome to PART 4 of my story. We started this part in the year 1965. I have moved around a bit and bought a house in the lovely heart of Louisiana, New Orleans.

Aliah and I would often take walks around the block, exploring the various corners of the city. In the time I was there, I came across a person of emotional flamboyance. During the week of Carnival, Aliah and I would usually stay in the house, but this time around, she convinced me to go. So, I came out of my house, and we enjoyed the festivities.

I chose to wear my black gold dress, with a veil to match it. I looked amazing as always, but that's not the point. When people were riding floats through the streets, I felt the presence of another god. Her name was Demmona Diamond.

She was extravagant, her float was like a star, and with a barrel in front of her full of diamonds, she would throw a handful of diamonds in the crowd grinning with her perfect teeth. She would say things like, "Take it, my lovelies, remember diamonds are forever," among other things.

She was so full of herself throwing diamonds around like it was nothing. She thought she was so perfect, and well, I had had enough of her and left.

"Are you sure we can't stay a little bit longer?" Aliah asked.

"No," I replied and took her back to the house.

Dark Clovers

I need a break from this documentary. I'm going to take a
walk.

Is she gone? Great, my lovely. Hello there, I am
Demmona Diamond, but most gods call me DD. I will
take over from here for a bit until she cools off.
I am the Goddess of Showmanship, Fame, and Riches.
They call me the party goddess, but who has time to list
how many significant events I have done.
We'll continue the story in New Orleans, and right after
that, float through the streets. I had decided that it would
be nice to visit a place of my own. A theatre that is, and
see how my worshippers were doing. You know, one
must always check on things. I was, prancing into the
theatre house in my beautiful black rhinestone dress with
my favorite black feather boa. As I observed the show

with great pleasure, I happened to spot a precious gem of

my own. His name was Finius Dartmouth. Such a

stunning beauty, almost as beautiful and unique as

myself. But we know that isn't possible, haha!

Regardless, I took a fancy to him, and we courted for a

few years until he finally asked to marry. Of course, I

turned him down, my lovely, a god can't marry a mortal.

It's like marrying dirt. But I did get 4 beautiful children

out of it. Emmy, Tony, Oscar, and Grammy. Boy, did

they take off quickly? They have events in their honor

now.

I would be lying if I said I wasn't a proud mother, but

apart from that, I have had my own problems with

mortals, and I have had my unique way to punish them.

One time, this one mortal man came to me a bit cross, he

thought himself above greatness, but little by little, his

Dark Clovers

wealth, fame, and reputation crumbled into the ground.

Now, all he can see is dirt and wood. I cursed those who

followed him to sing and dance for the rest of their lives

and stripped them from getting any recognition. Oh,

cheese and crackers, Eresabith is on her way back.

Toodles my lovely!

<u>*A Letter From The Author*</u>

Hi reader! I am your author Diana Dark, and I hope that you love my stories, but first let's get to know me a little. I was born in a land in the south called Georgia, however I spent most of my life in Texas in which I now know as home. In my early days, growing up as the youngest of three children, I always found ways to keep myself company in creating things. Usually because everyone else was busy and didn't have time to play with their little inteloper. However, I did enjoy going outside and playing with animals and bugs . I actually wanted to become a vet and help as many animals as possible, and I took time to learn all about

Dark Clovers

them and their peculiarities; Animal Planet became my best friend and a great teacher.

Everyday and everynight, I watched and learned all I could whenever I could. That is, of course, when I wasn't playing with my friends, doing annoying work books my parents gave me, or just creating worlds in my mind. But whenever I did those other things, I would always have music playing, whether it was music from the radio, from a cd or from my family singing together. I was labeled the living radio in my house because they could ask me about any song and I would sing it. The lesson was that if I heard it and I liked it, I put enough energy into learning the melody and lyrics all by ear, which helped me when I joined the choirs at my church and High School.

Still, for a good while, I wanted to be a vet, until the passion of creation of more material things took its place, and for a good few years, I applied myself to creating different wild things, sculptures, and buildings. My parents saw this and sought to grow such a gift and therefore, they gifted me with legos, clay and other art materials to feed my hunger for creation. With such things, I made vases, paintings, miniature models of famous architecture such as the leaning Tower of Pisa, The Seattle Space Needle, and so many other great things.

Soon enough when I was in high school, I entered into classes that best fit my passion of creating. However, like many things, writing became a natural setting for me, starting out with writing small stories in my english class to writing poems that were published in

Dark Clovers

books to actually writing short stories and creating

characters that many of those around me found

fascinating.

Mostly my life has been a great story of its own

and each moment I reached a resolution, one chapter to

another would begin to unfold before my very eyes. In

this small selection of stories, I wanted to explore many

avenues of some of what some would say uncommon

themes that have been used in familiar plots in film and

on paper. As for such, I wish to create an ongoing series

of some of these stories to better expound on certain

characters and also expand the worlds they are in. Maybe

even perhaps have some of the stories collide with one

another to create something magnificent.

With your help I will be able to create masterpieces for future readers to enjoy and inspire. Know that when you read my stories, I will try my best to pull from you emotions of all kinds, even some that don't have names yet. I want to make a good lasting impression upon you with my stories and when I do, I expect to welcome you back with either a continuation or a new story all together. Thank you for listening to me for a bit and I hope that you enjoyed the stories I have written. I hope they inspire you to write stories of your very own.

Dark Clovers

Diana Dark

www.ingramcontent.com/pod-product-compliance
Lightning Source LLC
Chambersburg PA
CBHW020118180626
46812CB00006B/2652